Mortals

Of

Kandahar

Acknowledgements

Writing this novel has been a journey of passion, introspection, and discovery, and it would not have been possible without the unwavering support of the incredible people in my life.

First and foremost, I am deeply grateful to my family—my husband, whose love, patience, and encouragement gave me the strength to bring this story to life.

To my parents.

A special thanks to my daughter, whose curiosity and joy remind me of the beauty of storytelling.

This novel owes its foundation to the timeless inspirations of history, culture, and human resilience. To the readers of my previous works, including Musings of Enkindled Heart, your love for my words fuels my creative spirit.

Finally, to you, my readers, thank you for allowing me to share this world with you. Your time, imagination, and trust mean more than words can express.

Synopsis

"Mortals of Kandahar" is a delightfully alluring tale of love, destiny, and the yearning for fulfillment amidst the intricate dance of tradition and ambition.

At the heart of this story is Kyra, a woman of rare grace and unbreakable integrity, whose beauty and intellect captivate all who cross her path. Her soul is a quiet storm-layered with loyalty, wisdom, and courage-and it is this magnetic essence that binds two men to her fate.

Aryanath, her enduring confidant, stands as the steady flame in her life, representing a love rooted in shared histories and gentle constancy. Yet Darius, a man of commanding presence and unwavering passion, finds himself ensnared by Kyra's brilliance and honesty. Drawn to her in ways he never imagined, Darius embarks on a journey of tender obsession, his desire for her igniting moments of undeniable intimacy that shimmer with an unspoken promise.

In the ancient city of Kandahar, where the whispers of history mingle with the pulse of ambition, Kyra, Aryanath, and Darius find themselves entwined in a delicate web of loyalty and longing. As their worlds collide, each must confront the boundaries of their own desires, questioning what it means to stay true to oneself in the face of undeniable passion and duty.

"Mortals of Kandahar" is a lyrical exploration of the human soul's most profound questions-how far will we go for love? What price do we pay for the paths we choose? And, when bound by both love and loyalty, can any heart remain truly untouched? This novel is a journey through the shadows and light of desire, a tale that lingers long after the final page is turned.

Table of Contents

Chapter 1 - The Scholars of Old Kandahar

The air in Old Kandahar was thick with the scent of ancient stone and ink. Inside the quiet chamber of the temple archives, Aryanath bent over his work, surrounded by the hushed echoes of history. The warm candlelight illuminated his fingers, steady and sure as he carved words in Prakrit onto a new scroll.

He wore a simple brown robe, but it carried the marks of a scholar-the ink stains on his sleeves, the worn leather of his writing pouch, and the gleam of intelligence in his eyes.

Aryanath was young, only twenty, yet his mind held more knowledge than most men twice his age. His father, a respected scribe of the temple, had spent years teaching him the sacred duty of preserving Kandahar's history. Aryanath knew the weight of his task. This city, once the heart of the Zunbil kingdom and a crossroads of cultures, was a living relic, containing fragments of every empire that had ever ruled it. From the inscriptions of the Mauryans to the faded scripts of the Greeks, each piece of writing was a story, a memory, and a truth that Aryanath was determined to protect.

One day, as Aryanath translated a passage from Ashoka's edicts, his mentor, Old Bhadrasen, entered the room with a purposeful silence. The elder's face was lined with age, each wrinkle a testament to a lifetime spent in service to history. He placed a gentle hand on Aryanath's shoulder, interrupting his work with a rare gesture of affection.

"You are too dedicated, Aryanath," Bhadrasen said, his voice like gravel softened by wisdom. "The edicts have waited centuries. They will not fade by tomorrow."

Aryanath smiled but did not pause in his work. "The world outside changes, master, but these words do not. They are worth the effort."

Bhadrasen chuckled, nodding. "True. But remember, history is not preserved only in ink and stone. It lives in the people who carry it forward."

Just then, Kyra, the princess of Alexander's temple, entered the chamber, her dark hair veiled by a fine cloth adorned with the emblem of the Greek hero.

Though her heritage was mixed, she held herself with the poise of a noblewoman, as if Alexander's blood ran through her veins. Her eyes, deep and guarded, studied Aryanath with a mix of curiosity and reverence.

"Forgive me for intruding, Aryanath," Kyra began,

"but I heard you were translating Ashoka's latest inscription. I wanted to see it before the court claims it."

Aryanath nodded, offering her a seat beside him.

Kyra's gaze lingered on the scrolls, her expression a blend of fascination and sorrow. "The great king Ashoka," she murmured. "To think that one man's words have survived where so many others are forgotten."

Her voice was filled with a wistful pride, a reminder of her connection to a distant heritage that the city itself seemed to share. Aryanath respected her deeply. She had been the one who, despite opposition from the elders, had fought to preserve Alexander's temple. It was a place both Greek and local citizens visited, a rare symbol of unity in an often-divided land. The temple was built around 3rd century. It was a cavern surrounded by several small stone buildings and connected with secret tunnels and chambers.

Kyra studied the inscription, her fingertips tracing the ancient Prakrit letters. "Sometimes I wonder, Aryanath, if all this will survive. Kandahar has seen too many wars, too many rulers. How much longer before our past is destroyed in the flames of conquest?"

Aryanath, usually measured and calm, felt a pang of the same fear. The city was again under threat, its strategic position making it desirable to the Seleucid Empire. News of approaching soldiers had trickled in, bringing with them whispers of war. And in times of war, scholars and scribes were often the first to be silenced.

"The words may be erased," Aryanath replied softly,

"but the memories will survive as long as someone remembers. Even in war, knowledge cannot be completely extinguished."

Bhadrasen looked at them both, his gaze proud yet tinged with sadness. "You two remind me of our duty.

Kandahar is more than land and stone; it is a living memory of empires past, a bridge between cultures." He paused, his eyes clouded with the knowledge of old scars. "We must do everything we can to keep it alive, even if we are the last to remember."

As night fell, Aryanath gathered his scrolls, feeling the weight of his purpose. The quiet chamber, with its scent of parchment and stone, seemed to breathe with him. He looked at Kyra, who stood by the doorway, a figure etched with the shadows of Alexander's legacy, and at Bhadrasen, a man whose lifetime had been dedicated to guarding Kandahar's truth.

Together, they were the keepers of Old Kandahar, scholars in a world that teetered on the edge of war.

As Aryanath blew out the candle, he whispered a silent vow to the city he loved-to remember, to protect, and to preserve, no matter the cost.

Chapter 2 - The Temple of Alexander

The sun rose over Old Kandahar, casting its first rays on the temple dedicated to Alexander the Great. The stone walls bore faint engravings, their edges softened by time, yet they still hinted at scenes of ancient battles, victories, and divine visions. The temple was a rare relic, a testament to the deep roots Alexander had planted in these lands centuries ago.

For Kyra, it was not just a place of worship-it was a reminder of her ancestors, a bridge between her Greek and Kandahari blood.

That morning, Kyra moved quietly through the temple's shadowed corridors, carrying a small bowl of sacred oils. She paused before the central statue of Alexander, its marble surface chipped in places but still exuding a commanding presence. She knelt, whispering a prayer she had learned from her grandmother, a prayer that invoked both Greek and local deities, a symbol of the harmonious blend her family had long upheld.

As she began her rituals, she was joined by Aryanath.

Though not a worshipper of Alexander, Aryanath had often come to the temple, finding a certain peace in its silence, its echoes of past civilizations. Today, however, he came with news.

"Kyra," he greeted softly, bowing his head in respect.

Kyra looked up, a trace of worry flitting across her face as she saw the urgency in his eyes. "What is it, Aryanath?"

"The Seleucid forces have reached the outskirts," Aryanath replied, his voice barely above a whisper.

"I overheard the temple elders speaking this morning. They fear that the city will be taken."

Kyra's heart sank, though she kept her composure.

For months, rumors had warned of the Seleucid advance. With its position as the gateway to both the Indian subcontinent and the Middle East, Kandahar was too strategic, too precious. But hearing it from Aryanath, whose knowledge was never idle gossip, made it real.

"What will happen to the temple?" she asked, her voice steady, though her hands gripped the edge of the altar.

Aryanath hesitated. He respected her devotion to Alexander's temple and knew it held a symbolic value to many in the city. But he also knew the harsh reality of war. The Seleucids were pragmatic conquerors; anything they considered unnecessary could be destroyed without a second thought.

"I don't know," he admitted. "The temple is a symbol of both cultures—perhaps they will see its worth. But we must be prepared for... other outcomes."

Kyra straightened, a fierce resolve hardening her gaze. "I won't let them take it without a fight."

Aryanath admired her spirit, though he knew her defiance could lead to consequences. "There may be a way to protect it without open resistance," he suggested, trying to offer a gentler path. "I could speak with Bhadrasen. He may be able to appeal to the city council, to remind them that the temple is a testament to Kandahar's history. Perhaps they could negotiate its preservation."

Kyra's expression softened. She knew Aryanath was right; direct confrontation was a risk she couldn't afford. And Bhadrasen's voice, as one of the city's respected scholars, might carry enough weight to sway the council.

"Very well," she agreed, her voice quieter. "But I will still prepare for the worst. There are sacred relics within these walls—if the city falls, we cannot let them be taken or destroyed."

Aryanath nodded, a plan forming in his mind.

"Perhaps we can create copies of the most important texts and relics," he offered. "The originals can be hidden. If the worst happens, we'll still have something to preserve."

Together, they spent the rest of the day in hushed preparations. Kyra led Aryanath to a hidden chamber in the temple, a narrow room carved deep into the earth where relics and scrolls of immeasurable value were kept. There were golden figurines of deities, intricately carved in both Greek and Kandahari styles, and ancient scrolls bearing the writings of priests, kings, and warriors. It was here, in this quiet chamber, that the history of Old Kandahar lay preserved.

With great care, Aryanath began copying sections of the most valuable scrolls. Kyra watched him, her mind racing with the implications. For generations, her family had kept these relics safe, bearing the responsibility of Alexander's legacy in a land that was as much hers as it was her ancestors'. She knew that with each conquest, her lineage's claim to this land weakened, yet her loyalty to Kandahar only grew stronger.

As night fell, Aryanath finished his work, his fingers aching from hours of writing. He glanced at Kyra, who had taken a small statue of Alexander and wrapped it carefully in a cloth.

"Where will you hide it?" he asked, nodding toward the statue.

Kyra looked at him, a bittersweet smile playing on her lips. "Beneath the altar," she replied. "My grandmother told me there's a compartment there, meant to keep sacred objects safe from intruders."

They walked to the altar together, each step heavy with the weight of their task. Kyra knelt and lifted the stone, revealing a small hollow space beneath.

She placed the statue inside, whispering a final prayer, her voice breaking slightly.

As she replaced the stone, she looked up at Aryanath, her expression fierce. "If Kandahar falls, this temple may fall with it. But our history will live on, in these copies, in our memories. We won't let them erase us."

Aryanath placed a reassuring hand on her shoulder, his own resolve matching hers. "We won't," he promised. "As long as there are people like you to remember, Kandahar will endure."

They stood together in the temple's dim light, two guardians of Old Kandahar, bound by their love for a city that was always under threat but had never truly fallen. Their lives, their work, and their heritage were now intertwined with the fate of this land.

Outside, the faint echo of distant drums began to rise, a foreboding rhythm in the still night air. The Seleucids were closer now, the shadow of conquest looming over Kandahar. But within the temple walls, Aryanath and Kyra made a silent vow to preserve their city's soul, no matter the price.

Chapter 3 - Zunbil's Sword

The fires of dawn cast an orange glow across Kandahar's eastern walls, where Rajvanta, a warrior of the Zunbil dynasty, stood overlooking the city he had sworn to protect. The Seleucid army was now a visible force on the horizon, a tide of steel and banners advancing slowly but steadily, like an impending storm.

Rajvanta's hand rested on the hilt of his sword, a weapon that had been passed down through generations of his family. Its blade was engraved with ancient symbols and stories of the Zunbils' ancestors, the kings who had ruled these lands long before any foreign empire had dared set foot here. It was more than a weapon—it was a piece of Kandahar's history, a reminder of the courage and resilience of his people.

Today, however, he felt the weight of his duty more heavily than ever. The thought of Kandahar falling, of its temples and sacred sites desecrated, filled him with a cold rage. His gaze drifted toward the Temple of Alexander in the distance, where he knew Kyra and Aryanath were working tirelessly to preserve what they could.

As if summoned by his thoughts, Aryanath approached, his face grim. The young scholar's presence on the battlements was unusual, and his expression told Rajvanta that he bore news.

"They're closer," Aryanath said quietly, his voice steady despite the fear that tightened his features.

"The temple is prepared, and Kyra has hidden some of the relics, but we're running out of time."

Rajvanta nodded, his jaw clenched. "This city has stood for centuries, Aryanath. It will not fall while I still have breath in my body."

Aryanath watched the warrior, his respect evident.

He knew that Rajvanta was more than a soldier; he was the embodiment of Kandahar's fighting spirit, a defender who had risked his life time and again for a land that had known no peace. The Zunbil dynasty was fading, and the people had become weary, yet Rajvanta stood resolute, an anchor for all who believed Kandahar could still survive.

"You know the odds are against us," Aryanath murmured, not as a challenge but as a plea for honesty.

Rajvanta's gaze hardened. "I do. But history remembers those who fought, not those who surrendered."

As they spoke, Bhadrasen arrived, leaning heavily on his walking staff, his face a mask of grim acceptance.

Though age had wearied him, he still carried the dignity of a scholar, a keeper of truth.

"I have lived long enough to see empires rise and fall," Bhadrasen said, his voice deep and resonant.

"Yet this city, this land, has endured. It is made of something far stronger than stone or steel. But, Rajvanta," he continued, turning to the warrior, "we must be wise as well as brave. If we are to survive, we must protect what we can."

Rajvanta glanced at his sword, the blade that had been forged in Kandahar's fires and wielded by his ancestors in battles long past. Its edge glinted in the morning light, a silent promise of retribution to any who would threaten his home.

"I will defend Kandahar," he said, lifting the sword and looking toward the approaching enemy. "And if they seek to destroy us, I will remind them that we are not a land easily conquered."

As the sun climbed higher, Rajvanta summoned his fellow warriors, men and women who had trained under the Zunbil banner and shared his loyalty. They gathered at the city's gates, their faces a mix of determination and fear, their eyes fixed on Rajvanta as he addressed them.

"Today, we stand not just for ourselves, but for all who came before us," he declared, his voice carrying across the courtyard. "For our ancestors, who forged this land, and for those who will come after us, who will inherit it. We are the defenders of Kandahar, and as long as one of us still stands, our city will live."

His words ignited a fire in their hearts, a shared understanding that this fight was not only for survival but for honor. Each soldier gripped their weapon with a renewed sense of purpose, and for a moment, the fear gave way to a collective strength, a bond forged through generations of loyalty to Kandahar.

Aryanath stayed at Rajvanta's side, feeling both humbled and inspired by the warrior's unbreakable spirit. He, too, had made a vow to protect Kandahar's legacy, and though he was not a fighter, he knew that he had a role to play.

"Rajvanta," Aryanath said quietly, "if the worst happens, and we cannot hold the walls, we must have a plan to preserve our knowledge. Perhaps there are ways to protect the scrolls, the artifacts, even if the city falls."

Rajvanta looked at Aryanath, a flicker of understanding in his gaze. "You are wise, Aryanath.

The sword may hold back the enemy, but it is the pen that keeps us alive long after the battle is over."

He turned to Bhadrasen, who nodded. "There is an old underground passage beneath the city," the elder said, his voice low. "It was built by the Zunbils as a refuge, a way to escape if the city was ever overrun. I suggest you use it to protect the artifacts, to carry Kandahar's legacy beyond these walls if necessary."

The plan took root among them, a silent agreement to protect the knowledge, the memory, even if it meant leaving the stones of Kandahar behind.

Rajvanta's eyes hardened as he prepared to fight, knowing that his sword would not only defend his city but also buy time for Aryanath and Kyra to secure its soul.

As the day wore on, the Seleucid army drew closer, their banners rippling in the wind, the rhythmic clang of metal echoing across the land. Rajvanta and his warriors prepared for the inevitable clash, their hearts steady, their spirits unbreakable. Aryanath withdrew to the temple, where Kyra awaited him, her face pale but resolute. Together, they began gathering the scrolls, statues, and relics, ready to move them through the hidden passage if the city fell.

And as night descended, the city held its breath, the air charged with anticipation. The citizens of Kandahar looked to Rajvanta, a warrior carrying the legacy of his ancestors, and to Aryanath and Kyra, guardians of the city's knowledge. They were the last line, the ones who stood between Kandahar and the darkness that threatened to erase it.

As Rajvanta took his place at the city's gates, sword in hand, he whispered a silent vow—to his ancestors, to Kandahar, to the warriors beside him. He would not let the city fall without a fight. Zunbil's sword would strike one final time, its blade a testament to a history that would endure, no matter the cost.

In the silence before the storm, Kandahar's defenders braced themselves, bound by duty, courage, and love for a land that would live in their hearts forever.

Chapter 4 - In the Shadow of Ashoka

The nights in Kandahar had grown tense, the air thick with the weight of looming war. Within the temple walls, Kyra and Aryanath moved swiftly, their hands careful as they gathered relics and scrolls, preparing them for the hidden passage that led to safety. The distant sounds of the Seleucid forces settling into their camps haunted the night, a reminder that time was running out.

Among the relics was one particularly precious artifact: a stone slab with an inscription written in both Greek and Prakrit, a testament from the time of Ashoka, the great Mauryan emperor. Known as the Kandahar Bilingual Rock Inscription, it bore the words of Ashoka's edicts, proclaiming messages of peace, tolerance, and unity. To Kyra and Aryanath, it was more than just a relic—it was a beacon of hope, a reminder that Kandahar had once been part of a larger world where respect and harmony held sway over conquest and division.

Kyra gently traced her fingers over the engraved letters, her thoughts drifting to stories she had heard as a child. Her grandmother had often spoken of Ashoka's transformation, how he had renounced violence after the horrors of the Kalinga War, and how he had chosen the path of dharma, spreading messages of compassion across his empire. That Ashoka had left a mark here in Kandahar was a source of pride for many in the city, a reminder of the legacy of wisdom and strength their land held.

"Kyra," Aryanath's voice broke through her reverie.

He was watching her, his expression solemn. "This inscription... it's more than a relic. It's a reminder of what we stand for. If the Seleucids knew its significance, they might respect it."

Kyra looked at him, her heart heavy. "Or they might see it as a symbol of defiance and destroy it," she replied. "But we cannot risk losing it. This stone connects us to a time when peace was possible, even among empires. It deserves to survive, even if we do not."

Aryanath nodded. He knew the inscription's value, not only as a historical artifact but as a

representation of Kandahar's soul—a city that had known the touch of multiple cultures and had retained its own unique identity through it all. They would have to protect it, just as fiercely as they protected the temple.

Meanwhile, Rajvanta prepared his warriors outside, making last-minute plans with Bhadrasen. The older scholar had served as a quiet advisor to the Zunbil dynasty for decades and held an encyclopedic knowledge of Kandahar's history. He was frail now, but his mind was sharp, and he sensed the weight of history pressing upon them.

"Rajvanta," Bhadrasen said, placing a hand on the warrior's shoulder. "Before you draw your sword, remember what it is you're defending. Ashoka taught that true power lies not in force, but in principle. We are fighting for more than a city—we are fighting for a way of life, a legacy."

Rajvanta looked at the elder, absorbing his words. As a warrior, his first instinct was to fight, to push back the invaders with all his might. But Bhadrasen's reminder gave him pause. It wasn't just the stones of Kandahar he wanted to protect, but the ideals and values that had defined his people for centuries.

Kandahar was not only a city; it was a testament to resilience, wisdom, and the power of knowledge and belief.

"I understand, Bhadrasen," he said, his voice quiet but resolute. "I fight for Kandahar, but I also fight to preserve the spirit of Ashoka, and all who came before him. As long as I draw breath, that spirit will not be extinguished."

Later that evening, Rajvanta sought Kyra and Aryanath within the temple. He wanted to see the inscription for himself, to remind himself of the legacy he was about to defend. As he stood before the stone, his fingers brushing the ancient words, he felt a surge of determination. The message of peace carved by Ashoka had survived centuries, yet today it faced a very different kind of battle.

"Kyra, Aryanath," Rajvanta began, turning to them with a steady gaze, "if Kandahar's walls fall, I want you to take this inscription and the scrolls with you.

Protect them as if they were your own lives. Let them be the testament of what we stood for."

Kyra looked at him, her eyes bright with both fear and determination. "We will, Rajvanta. This stone, these words... they are a reminder that even in the darkest times, we can choose light."

The three of them shared a quiet moment, united by the knowledge that they were guardians of Kandahar's soul. They each had their role to play, and none of them took it lightly.

As dawn broke, the Seleucid forces made their first move, their banners filling the horizon, their soldiers forming ranks. The city's defenses were outmatched, and the citizens of Kandahar braced for a brutal siege. Rajvanta, at the forefront, raised Zunbil's sword, his heart pounding with a mixture of fear and resolve. He was not only defending a city; he was defending history itself.

From the temple, Kyra and Aryanath watched as Rajvanta led his warriors. They whispered a prayer to the gods, hoping that Ashoka's spirit, his legacy of peace and resilience, would somehow protect them.

As the first sounds of battle erupted, Kyra took a deep breath, turning to Aryanath.

"It's time," she said, her voice steady. "We must secure the relics and prepare for the worst."

Together, they carefully wrapped the inscription in layers of cloth, whispering words of reverence as they secured it. The relics, the scrolls, each piece of Kandahar's history-these were treasures worth protecting, no matter the cost.

As they descended into the hidden passage, carrying the weight of Kandahar's history with them, they heard the distant clanging of swords, the cries of battle. Rajvanta's voice rose above the fray, a rallying call that echoed through the temple walls. He fought not only with strength but with conviction, his actions a testament to the teachings of Ashoka, who

had once ruled these lands with a vision of unity and compassion.

In the shadow of Ashoka's legacy, Kyra, Aryanath, and Rajvanta stood as the final guardians of a city that had endured centuries of turmoil, a city that refused to be forgotten. As long as one of them remained, the spirit of

Kandahar would survive, carrying forward the values that Ashoka had once etched into the stones of this ancient land.

The hidden passage beneath the temple was known only to the most trusted within Kandahar's inner circle. Centuries before, artisans and priests had carved it into the limestone foundation, creating a network of winding paths that extended deep into the earth. Built as both a sanctuary and a safeguard for Kandahar's most treasured relics, the passage was a testament to the city's history and the wisdom of its ancestors.

The entrance lay behind a concealed wall within the innermost chamber of the temple, where an intricately carved relief of a lotus flower marked the way. To the untrained eye, it was just another part of the temple's decor, blending seamlessly with the ancient stone. But for those who knew its secret, a gentle press against the lotus's center would release a hidden latch, opening a narrow, dark corridor that descended steeply into the ground.

Kyra and Aryanath carefully navigated the passage, their footsteps echoing faintly in the silence. Torches in hand, they moved forward cautiously, the light casting flickering shadows along the damp stone walls. The air grew cooler as they descended, carrying with it the scent of age and stillness.

After several turns, they arrived at a small chamber, its walls lined with alcoves carved to hold sacred items.

Here, they carefully placed the relics they'd gathered-the scrolls, the inscriptions, and artifacts bearing Ashoka's teachings. The stone slab bearing the Greek and Prakrit edicts was given a central place in the chamber, resting on a pedestal that had been carved long ago, perhaps in anticipation of such a moment.

In the dim light, Kyra paused, taking in the sight of the relics now hidden away from the threat above.

This sanctuary represented more than just a hiding place; it was a vault for the soul of Kandahar, holding the knowledge and values that had shaped the city's identity.

"Do you think they'll be safe here?" Aryanath asked, his voice filled with both hope and worry.

Kyra nodded slowly. "This place has kept our ancestors' secrets safe for generations. If any place can protect them, it is here. As long as even one of us remembers its location, Kandahar's spirit will survive."

Together, they secured the chamber, layering it with stones and clay to mask its entrance and disguise any sign of disturbance. With one last look, they whispered silent prayers, hoping that, someday, these relics might see the light again and tell their stories to future generations.

With their task complete, they left the hidden passage, carrying with them the weight of Kandahar's legacy-now secured, but waiting for a future where peace would once again reign.

Chapter 5 - Secrets of the Herbalist

The siege of Kandahar had stretched into days, the sound of clashing swords and the cries of the wounded permeating the air. Despite the relentless advance of the Seleucid forces, Rajvanta and his warriors held firm, driven by a fierce loyalty to their land and its history. Yet with each passing hour, their strength waned, and the reality of dwindling resources weighed heavily on the defenders.

Hidden away in a secluded part of the city, Kyra and Aryanath continued their mission to protect Kandahar's relics. They had hidden the precious inscriptions and scrolls deep within the temple's underground passages, but Kyra knew their efforts might still be in vain if the city fell. She was no stranger to Kandahar's struggles-her family's lineage traced back through generations of herbalists, and she had learned the arts of healing and survival from her mother.

It was these teachings that had brought her to Mira, Kandahar's herbalist, an elder whose wisdom and knowledge of the region's flora had saved countless lives over the years. Mira's home was tucked within a small grove of trees, a sanctuary filled with plants that thrived even in the harshest conditions. The herbs she cultivated were the heart of her healing practice, and her knowledge was invaluable to the defenders of Kandahar.

Kyra entered Mira's home, her face set with determination. Mira was waiting, seated among drying bundles of herbs that filled the air with their earthy scent. Her eyes, sharp and perceptive despite her age, met Kyra's with a look of understanding.

"I know why you're here," Mira said softly, gesturing for Kyra to sit. "The city's strength is waning, and the soldiers need more than just courage to keep fighting."

Kyra nodded. "Rajvanta and his warriors are holding the line, but they're exhausted. The wounded are growing in number, and our supplies are running low. We need anything you can offer, Mira."

The herbalist gave a slow nod, considering Kyra's words. "There are plants here that most would overlook, remedies hidden in plain sight. Many in Kandahar have forgotten these ancient ways, but knowledge is as powerful as any weapon. Come with me, child."

Mira led Kyra into the grove, stopping before a patch of low-growing plants with delicate white flowers.

She knelt down, pulling one from the soil and carefully showing Kyra the roots. "This is ashwagandha," she explained. "It gives strength to the weary and calm to the anxious. It will help the soldiers withstand their exhaustion."

31

Kyra watched, absorbing every word as Mira continued her lesson. They moved from plant to plant-turmeric for wounds, neem for infections, holy basil for fever. Mira taught Kyra the preparation methods, the combinations that would yield the most potent results. Kyra's hands moved swiftly, her instincts honed by years of practice, and she felt a renewed purpose. These herbs were the hidden strengths of Kandahar, secrets passed down through generations, and they would help sustain the city's defenders.

Mira turned to Kyra with a final instruction. "There is one more herb you need to know," she said, her voice lowering. "It is rare and difficult to find, but in times like these, it may be our greatest ally. It is called sarpagandha. Its properties are potent—it can calm the heart, ease the mind, even bring peace to the suffering."

Kyra looked at her, realizing the weight of the knowledge Mira was passing down. Sarpagandha was considered one of the most powerful medicinal herbs in the region, known for its calming effects. If the siege continued, this herb could be the difference between life and death for many.

"Mira," Kyra said, her voice filled with gratitude, "I can't thank you enough. Your knowledge is a gift to Kandahar."

The herbalist smiled, her expression softened by years of compassion. "This city has given me life and purpose. To share what I know is only a small offering in return."

As Kyra gathered the herbs, Mira placed a hand on her shoulder. "Take care of yourself as well, child.

You bear the weight of Kandahar's history and its future. Remember, the knowledge you carry is as precious as any relic. Guard it well."

With her supplies bundled, Kyra returned to the temple, where Aryanath was waiting. His face brightened as he saw the array of herbs she carried, and together, they set to work preparing tinctures and poultices to aid the wounded.

As night fell, they distributed the remedies to the city's defenders. Rajvanta was among the first to receive the ashwagandha tincture, which Kyra explained would help him withstand the strain of battle. He took it gratefully, his respect for Kyra deepening with every interaction. Her quiet strength and knowledge had become as crucial to their resistance as any weapon.

As he sipped the bitter potion, Rajvanta turned to Kyra. "You carry the strength of Kandahar's spirit, Kyra. Your knowledge, your dedication... it reminds me of why we're fighting."

Kyra's gaze softened. "This city is more than just walls, Rajvanta. It's the people, the knowledge, the heritage. Each plant, each remedy holds the story of those who came before us. They are our allies, too."

The siege dragged on, but with the herbal remedies, the defenders found renewed resilience. Soldiers who had been on the verge of collapse regained strength, wounds that had begun to fester healed faster, and the spirit of the city endured. Kyra's knowledge had become a lifeline, a reminder that even in the darkest times, Kandahar's secrets could sustain them.

One evening, as Kyra and Aryanath tended to the wounded, Rajvanta entered the temple, a rare smile on his face. "The Seleucids are slowing," he announced. "They didn't expect us to last this long. I think... I think they're starting to doubt themselves."

Aryanath looked up, hope flickering in his eyes.

"Then we have a chance?"

Rajvanta nodded. *"A chance, yes. But it will still require all our strength and unity. We are not yet safe."*

As the days wore on, the knowledge of Mira's herbs became a cherished resource, a source of strength in the face of overwhelming odds. Kyra and Aryanath continued their work, sharing remedies and wisdom with those around them, while Rajvanta led the warriors with unwavering resolve.

And amid the relentless struggle, Kandahar's spirit endured-not just through the strength of its warriors, but through the resilience of its people, the secrets of its land, and the knowledge that, as long as they held onto their heritage, Kandahar could never truly fall.

In the shadows of siege and battle, the ancient wisdom of the herbalist guided them, a silent force that empowered Kandahar to hold fast. As long as they protected their knowledge and each other, the city's heart would continue to beat, a symbol of resistance and unity that no invader could extinguish.

Chapter 6 – The Merchant's Bargain

Kandahar's streets had become perilous as the siege wore on, its citizens growing weary and desperate.

Supplies dwindled, food became scarce, and each day brought fresh rumors of defeat or surrender. The city, once a thriving hub of culture and trade, now echoed with a tense silence broken only by distant battle cries and whispered conversations among those trying to survive.

In the midst of the turmoil, a figure moved through the alleys with a quiet confidence, his cloak wrapped tightly around him. Darius, a seasoned merchant known for his cunning and resourcefulness, had built his life on reading people and finding value where others saw none. He had traveled from Persia to the Indian subcontinent, trading spices, textiles, and jewels, amassing a small fortune along the way.

But with the siege's unrelenting grip, his connections had been cut off, and his influence was now limited to the narrow paths within the besieged city.

Darius's path led him to the temple, where he had been summoned for a meeting with Kyra and Aryanath.

Though he was well aware of the danger, Darius was intrigued. He had heard whispers about the relics hidden within the temple and was curious about what role he might play in their protection-or, perhaps, their negotiation. Even now, with the city's future uncertain, Darius saw an opportunity, one that might secure not only his survival but perhaps a gain even greater than riches.

Entering the temple, Darius found Kyra and Aryanath waiting for him in the shadows. They were visibly exhausted, yet their determination was unmistakable. Rajvanta had briefed them earlier, cautioning that while Darius's loyalty was questionable, his knowledge of the trade routes and influence within the city's underground could be vital in acquiring the supplies they so desperately needed.

Kyra stepped forward, meeting Darius's keen gaze.

"Thank you for coming, Darius. We are in need of... assistance, and we believe you're the only one who can provide it."

Darius inclined his head, his eyes narrowing as he assessed her words. "Assistance, yes? These are difficult times, Kyra. Assistance does not come cheaply. I'm risking a great deal simply by being here."

Aryanath spoke up, his tone calm but firm. "And we're aware of that. You've built your life on knowing the pulse of this city, its secrets and hidden paths. We need someone who can bring supplies through without attracting attention. The city's resources are thinning. You must know where the hidden stores are."

Darius considered this, his fingers tapping rhythmically against the hilt of a small dagger.

"You're asking a great deal. Smuggling supplies during a siege is no small task. But tell me, what do you have to offer in return? What assurance do I have that my risk will be rewarded?"

Kyra took a deep breath, realizing that this was no ordinary negotiation. Darius respected only two things: power and value. She decided to take a different approach, something that might appeal to the merchant's curiosity.

"Darius," she said, "do you know what lies beneath this temple?"

He raised an eyebrow, intrigued but cautious. "I've heard rumors, relics... artifacts of some worth, perhaps?"

Kyra nodded, choosing her words carefully. "More than mere artifacts. They are treasures that carry the history of Kandahar-ancient relics that tie our city to the reign of Ashoka and beyond. In the right hands, they could be priceless."

Darius's eyes flickered with interest. For a moment, the image of untold wealth danced before him. But he was a seasoned negotiator and knew better than to show his hand too soon.

"So, you're saying these relics are... available to me?" he asked, his tone laced with skepticism.

Aryanath interjected. "We're saying that, if you help us, we will ensure you are rewarded-not with wealth, but with knowledge and connections to a lineage that few can claim. We can provide you access to the archives of our history, something more valuable than gold to those who understand its worth."

Darius paused, weighing the offer. Knowledge had its own kind of power, particularly in a city as ancient and storied as Kandahar. If he were to secure the trust of these guardians, his influence could extend beyond mere goods and coin.

After a long silence, Darius spoke, his voice softened by a hint of respect. "Very well. I will secure the supplies you need. But know this— I am no fool. If I am betrayed or if I sense any hint of deceit, I will take my leave, and no one will be able to bring me back."

Kyra and Aryanath exchanged glances, relieved yet wary. They had won his cooperation, but the merchant was as dangerous as he was valuable. They could only hope that their alliance would hold

Over the following days, Darius moved skillfully through Kandahar's streets, slipping in and out of hidden passages and unguarded alleys. Through his network of contacts, he acquired sacks of grain, medicinal herbs, and weaponry-all items essential to the city's defense and survival. The goods were smuggled into the temple at night, hidden among crates labeled with less conspicuous items.

As Darius continued his work, he found himself drawn into the heart of Kandahar's resistance. His initial desire for wealth and influence gave way to a grudging respect for the people he was helping. The resilience of Rajvanta and his warriors, the quiet strength of Kyra and Aryanath as they tended to the wounded, the whispered prayers of citizens who refused to abandon hope-all of it stirred something within him, something he had long thought buried.

One evening, as Darius delivered a final batch of supplies, Rajvanta himself came to thank him. The warrior's face was stern, but his eyes held a hint of gratitude.

"Darius," Rajvanta said, "you have given us more than supplies. You have given us a chance to keep Kandahar's spirit alive. For that, we are indebted to you."

Darius nodded, accepting the thanks with a humility that surprised even himself. "I have simply done what was necessary," he replied, his voice low. "But perhaps there is more worth in Kandahar than I first imagined."

Kyra approached, her eyes meeting his with a rare look of warmth. "If Kandahar survives, you will be part of its story. And in that story, you will not be forgotten."

For a moment, Darius felt something unfamiliar—a connection, a sense of belonging to something greater than himself. It was fleeting, but it left a mark, and he knew that he had, in some way, become tied to Kandahar's fate.

As he turned to leave, Kyra called out to him. "One more thing, Darius."

He paused, looking back with curiosity.

"Legends say that Alexander himself once walked these streets," she continued, "and that he believed Kandahar to be a city worth preserving. Now, centuries later, it is in our hands. But without your help, our story might have ended before it even began."

Darius gave her a small, almost reluctant smile.

"Perhaps Kandahar has a way of capturing even the most unwilling of hearts. May it live to see another dawn."

With that, the merchant disappeared into the shadows, leaving behind the supplies that would sustain Kandahar for a little longer. His bargain had been struck, his role sealed. Yet, in the quiet of the temple, Kyra, Aryanath, and Rajvanta understood that Darius had given them something far more valuable than mere goods.

In his own way, the merchant had brought hope-an invaluable gift in the darkest of times.

Chapter 7 - The Merchant's Heart

Darius's feelings for Kyra began as an admiration, fueled by the strength and determination he saw in her. She was a woman of both quiet resolve and fiery courage, a rare combination that he hadn't encountered before in his dealings across empires.

But over time, those feelings deepened into something more, something he had not anticipated.

One evening, as they worked together near the temple; in the cavern, carefully arranging the newly smuggled supplies, Darius found himself drawn to her in a way he could no longer resist. The flickering candle light cast a warm glow across her face, illuminating her focused gaze as she worked, her brow furrowed in thought. It was in these moments, in the quiet dedication she showed for Kandahar, that Darius felt his heart surrender completely.

"Kyra," he said softly, breaking the silence.

She looked up, her eyes meeting his, curious but unguarded. "Yes, Darius?"

For a moment, he was silent, as if weighing his words. "I never thought I'd find myself tied to a place like this, bound not by fortune or gain, but by... something more."

Kyra's gaze softened, sensing the sincerity in his voice. She knew the merchant well enough by now to understand that these words were not spoken lightly.

"Kandahar has a way of doing that, doesn't it?" she replied gently. "It takes hold of us, binds us to its fate, even when we least expect it."

Darius stepped closer, his hand hovering near hers.

"It's not just Kandahar, Kyra," he murmured, his voice barely a whisper. "It's you."

For a heartbeat, time seemed to stand still. The weight of his confession hung in the air between them, as tangible as the relics hidden beneath the temple. Kyra's breath caught, a mixture of surprise and something unspoken flickering in her eyes. She had always admired Darius's resilience, his cleverness in the face of danger. But in this moment, she saw another side of him—a vulnerability, a longing she hadn't expected.

The distance between them disappeared, and for a brief moment, the world outside the temple faded away. Darius's hand brushed against hers, his touch warm and electric. His eyes held hers with an intensity that made her pulse quicken, and before she could stop herself, she felt her own heart stirring in response.

But just as quickly, Kyra's mind returned to Aryanath, the warrior who had been her steadfast companion through Kandahar's darkest days.

Aryanath, who had fought by her side, who understood the depth of her commitment to their city and its people. She was torn between two men, each possessing qualities that drew her in different ways:

Aryanath with his loyalty and strength, Darius with his passion and mystery.

Sensing her hesitation, Darius pulled back, his expression laced with a hint of sadness. He knew that she was not his to claim, that her heart was bound to something larger than any one person. Yet, he couldn't deny the connection between them, nor the love that had blossomed within him, unbidden and undeniable.

"Forgive me, Kyra," he whispered, his voice filled with regret. "I didn't mean to overstep."

Kyra reached out, touching his arm softly, her eyes meeting his with a mixture of gratitude and sorrow.

"You've given Kandahar a chance, Darius. And... you've given me something I cannot name, but that I will always carry with me."

As Darius left the temple that night, he felt the weight of his love for her, a love that would remain unspoken, yet forever a part of him. He had fallen deeply, irrevocably in love with a woman who might never be his, captivated by her integrity, her intelligence, her fierce loyalty. In her, he had found something he had long sought: a reason to care, a reason to fight, even in a city torn by war.

But the shadow of Aryanath lingered between them, a reminder of the man who had known Kyra far longer, who shared a history with her that Darius could not erase. And so, Darius resolved to remain by her side, to protect her and Kandahar in whatever way he could, even if his love would forever remain a silent, unfulfilled longing.

Chapter 8 - A Vision of Flames

The weeks that followed were fraught with tension as Kandahar braced itself for the inevitable siege.

Darius, Kyra, and Aryanath worked tirelessly within the temple, fortifying their defenses and preparing for what they knew could be their final stand. Each passing day deepened the bond between the three of them, yet an unspoken tension lingered in the air, thickening like the smoke that began to waft from distant fires.

Darius had thrown himself into the task of securing the temple and the relics within, but his thoughts often strayed to Kyra. He noticed how her laughter sparkled like sunlight, how her fierce resolve brought hope to those around her. She had become not just a beacon for the people of Kandahar, but also the object of his most cherished dreams. However, he felt the distance grow as Aryanath remained a steadfast presence by her side, ever the protective warrior and confidant.

One evening, after a long day of preparations, Kyra found herself alone on the temple's balcony, looking out over the city that had become her life. The horizon was awash in hues of red and gold as the sun set, but beneath the beauty lay a foreboding darkness. She could feel the weight of uncertainty in the air, the palpable tension as if the world itself was holding its breath.

Darius approached quietly, his presence a welcome distraction from her worries. "You should take a moment to breathe, Kyra," he said, his voice low and soothing. "Even the strongest of us need a respite."

Kyra turned to him, a soft smile gracing her lips. "It's hard to find peace when the flames of war are so close," she replied, gesturing toward the horizon.

"But I appreciate your concern, Darius."

As they stood side by side, the setting sun painted their features in a warm glow, and Kyra felt a familiar pull toward him. There was something magnetic in the way he looked at her, as if he could see into her very soul. The tension between them surged again, stronger than before, and Kyra felt the flicker of longing deep within her.

"Do you believe we'll win this fight?" Darius asked, breaking the silence.

"I must," she replied firmly. "For the sake of our people, for Kandahar's future."

Darius studied her, captivated by her fierce loyalty.

"You are more than just a warrior, Kyra. You embody the spirit of this city. It is your heart that gives them hope."

Kyra felt a flush of warmth at his words, a flutter of something she had tried to deny. "You've been a part of that spirit too, Darius. Your courage in these trying times has inspired many."

As they stood there, the distant sounds of battle rang out, a reminder of the world outside their moment of stillness. Yet, for Darius, the noise faded as he took a step closer to Kyra. "I want you to know that, no matter what happens, I will always stand by you."

Kyra met his gaze, her heart racing as she felt the unspoken connection between them. But before she could respond, a flicker of movement caught her eye.

A figure appeared in the doorway-Aryanath, his expression tense and determined.

"Kyra, Darius," he called, interrupting their moment.

"We need to finalize our plans for tonight. The enemy is drawing closer, and we must be prepared."

Darius stepped back, the tension in the air dissipating like the final rays of the sun. Aryanath's arrival felt like a chasm opening between him and Kyra, a reminder of the complexities of their situation.

"Of course," Kyra said, her voice steadier than she felt. "Let's gather everyone."

As they moved back inside, Darius felt a rush of frustration. He was growing more deeply in love with Kyra each day, but he also knew that Aryanath held a significant place in her heart. The love triangle tightened around him, each day blurring the lines between friendship, loyalty, and desire.

Later that night, as the fires from the encroaching enemy flickered ominously on the horizon, Darius stood on the temple steps, staring out into the darkness. He could feel the weight of his unexpressed feelings for Kyra pressing against his chest, a fire that refused to be extinguished.

The night air was thick with anticipation, and as he prepared to join Kyra and Aryanath for their final strategy meeting, a vision flashed through his mind.

He saw flames engulfing Kandahar, the city he had come to love, its beauty and strength reduced to ashes. He saw himself standing beside Kyra, reaching out for her, only to find her slipping through his fingers like smoke.

Shaken by the intensity of the vision, Darius closed his eyes, forcing himself to breathe through the panic. He couldn't let that vision come to pass. He needed to protect her, to ensure that the love blooming between them didn't wither away in the face of destruction.

As they gathered with the others, the weight of their impending battle loomed over them like a dark cloud. Aryanath led the discussion with fierce resolve, his voice steady and commanding. But Darius could see the way Kyra leaned closer to Aryanath, how their shared history forged an invisible bond that he could never break.

Yet, amidst the chaos, Darius resolved to fight not only for Kandahar but for Kyra as well. He would lay bare his feelings when the time was right. He would show her that love, like flames, could ignite and consume, but it could also warm and illuminate, giving strength in the darkest of times.

As the night deepened, Darius found himself glancing at Kyra from across the room, her spirit shining even in the face of danger. He knew he couldn't let the moment pass without trying to reach her heart, to claim his place beside her. Whatever the outcome, he would not let fear of failure keep him silent.

In the flickering light of the mashal torches, amidst the strategizing and hushed whispers, a fierce determination ignited within him. Darius would face the flames of war, not only as a merchant but as a man ready to fight for love. The dawn would come, and with it, the promise of a new beginning for Kandahar-and perhaps a chance for him and Kyra to forge a path together, illuminated by their shared passion and unyielding hope.

Chapter 9 - The Battle of Arachosia

The dawn of the Battle of Arachosia broke with an eerie stillness, the air heavy with anticipation and dread. The sun cast a pale light over the city of Kandahar, illuminating the fortifications that had been hastily erected around the temple. As Darius, Aryanath, and Kyra prepared for the onslaught, the weight of their impending fight pressed upon them like a shroud.

The strategy they had crafted was fraught with danger, but Darius was determined to see it through.

He could feel Kyra's eyes on him, her silent support bolstering his resolve. Yet, with every passing moment, the unspoken tension between them pulsed in the air, a reminder of their shared connection that grew deeper with each danger they faced.

The air crackled with tension as the sun dipped low on the horizon, casting long shadows over the battlefield of Arachosia. Warriors from Kandahar, brave and steadfast, had gathered, preparing for a conflict that threatened not only their land but also their very existence. The call to arms had echoed through the city, and now, as Darius surveyed the camp, he felt the weight of responsibility pressing heavily on his shoulders.

Reports had come in that Rajvanta, one of the most skilled commanders of their forces, had been seriously wounded in the skirmish that had unfolded just hours before. The men were demoralized, their spirits waning without their leader to rally them.

Darius knew that the weapon supplies he was entrusted with were crucial to turning the tide of the battle. Without them, the warriors would be left vulnerable against the well-armed forces of their adversaries.

With a grim resolve, Darius donned his armor, the metallic pieces clinking softly as he secured each strap. He glanced at Kyra, who stood nearby, her face a mask of concern. She could see the determination in his eyes, but the uncertainty of the situation loomed large.

"Promise me you'll be careful," she implored, her voice low yet urgent. "We cannot lose you too."

Darius reached for her, taking her hands in his, feeling the warmth of her touch. "I will return, Kyra.

I swear it. For you, for Kandahar, and for our future." His words hung in the air, a vow wrapped in hope, yet he could sense the unspoken fears swirling between them.

As he moved toward the gathering warriors, Darius steeled himself for the task ahead. The men were waiting, their faces lined with anxiety, their eyes scanning the horizon for signs of trouble. He raised his voice, projecting confidence. "Listen to me! We are Kandahar! Our strength lies in our unity, in our courage. Today, we will not falter. The supplies I bring will give us the edge we need. We will fight for our land, for our families, and for each other!"

His words ignited a spark of hope among them, and as the murmurs of agreement spread, Darius felt a surge of adrenaline. With a final nod of encouragement, he mounted his horse, the animal snorting in anticipation, and set off toward the front lines.

The ride through the rugged terrain was treacherous, the path littered with remnants of past skirmishes.

As Darius galloped forward, the sounds of clashing swords and the cries of warriors grew louder, enveloping him in a cacophony of battle. He pushed himself harder, urgency driving him onward. Every second counted; every moment spent delaying their advance could cost them lives.

When he finally arrived at the frontline, chaos reigned. The clash of metal on metal filled the air, mingling with the shouts of warriors as they engaged the enemy. Darius quickly dismounted and joined the fray, his sword drawn and his instincts sharp. He weaved through the chaos, delivering powerful strikes and rallying the troops around him.

As he fought, his heart raced not only from the thrill of combat but also from the urgency of his mission.

He had to reach Rajvanta and deliver the supplies that would turn the tide. He could see the commander, surrounded by a group of warriors, struggling to maintain control as he fought against two opponents. The sight ignited a fire within Darius.

Pushing through the melee, Darius reached Rajvanta's side just as a fierce blow landed against the commander's shoulder, causing him to stumble back. Darius swiftly dispatched the attacker with a powerful strike, his blade slicing through the air with lethal precision.

"Rajvanta!" Darius shouted, concern flooding his voice as he knelt beside the commander, assessing his wounds. "We need to get you to safety!"

Rajvanta's breath was labored, but his eyes were fierce. "No... the men need me. We cannot lose this ground."

Darius shook his head, urgency lacing his words.

"You are not going to help anyone if you bleed out here. The supplies..." He gestured to the barrels nearby, "They're here! We can turn this battle if we act quickly."

With grim determination, Rajvanta nodded, accepting the reality of his situation. "Then let's do it.

Together."

Together, they rallied the remaining warriors, distributing the weapons and munitions among them. As the men armed themselves, a renewed energy surged through the ranks. Darius could feel the shift in morale, the warriors standing taller, their resolve igniting anew.

With Rajvanta back on his feet-albeit unsteady— they rejoined the fray, leading their warriors forward. The sound of clashing metal surged around them as the tides of battle began to turn. Darius fought with fervor, each strike a testament to his determination to protect those he loved.

In the midst of the chaos, however, he could not shake the nagging worry that tugged at his heart.

Kyra's face flashed before him, her concern etched in his mind. He fought not only for Kandahar but for her, for their future.

Just as victory seemed to edge closer, a sudden cry erupted from the other side of the battlefield. Darius turned to see a fierce warrior charging toward him, a figure cloaked in darkness, brandishing a sword that gleamed menacingly in the fading light. Darius steeled himself, readying his stance. This would be the moment that defined not only his fate but also the future of Kandahar.

With a battle cry that echoed through the chaos, Darius lunged forward, ready to confront the darkness head-on. In the clash of swords and the roar of battle, he fought not just for survival but for hope— a hope that would lead him back to Kyra, back to the life they were building together.

In the midst of the fight, he felt the bond they shared stronger than ever. As the battle raged on, Darius knew he would face whatever challenges lay ahead, not only for himself but for the love that fueled his spirit-the love that would guide him home.

As the enemy approached, a cacophony of shouts and clashing weapons erupted around them. The battlefield transformed into a swirling chaos of dust, sweat, and blood. Darius fought fiercely, adrenaline coursing through him, each strike fueled by the thought of protecting Kyra and the city they loved.

Amidst the fray, Darius's thoughts were a tangle of urgency and longing. He moved with purpose, ensuring that supplies reached the front lines, but the sound of clashing steel and the cries of battle threatened to drown out everything else. Just as he delivered a fresh supply of weapons to a struggling contingent of soldiers, he felt a sharp pain in his side.

He staggered back, clutching his wound, his vision blurring as he tried to comprehend what had just happened. A soldier had lunged at him, a blade flashing in the chaotic melee, and now blood flowed freely from the gash. Panic surged through him as he collapsed to the ground, the world around him fading into a haze.

As Darius lay there, his breaths shallow and rapid, his thoughts turned to Kyra. The image of her strong, fierce face haunted him as he struggled to remain conscious. Would he ever have the chance to tell her how he felt? Would he survive to see her again?

Meanwhile, Kyra was in the midst of her own battle

—a battle of heart and spirit. She fought with all her might, but her thoughts kept drifting back to Darius.

When she got to know about him getting injured, her heart dropped, fear gripping her chest like a vice.

"Darius!" she screamed, while the throng of soldiers carried him to the front of the temple. As she knelt beside him, the chaos of battle faded into the background, and the world narrowed down to just the two of them.

"Stay with me," she urged, her voice trembling as she pressed her hands against the wound, trying to stem the blood flow. "Please, don't leave me."

He looked up at her, his eyes flickering with pain but still holding that spark of life. "Kyra... I-" he struggled to say, but the words caught in his throat.

"Shh," she whispered, tears blurring her vision. "Just hold on. I'm here. You're not alone." She felt the weight of their unspoken love between them, and she prayed fervently, her heart pounding in time with the battle cries that surrounded them. "Please, let him live. Let me have him back."

Hours felt like days as the battle raged on. Darius slipped in and out of consciousness, each time returning to Kyra's unwavering presence, her fierce determination grounding him in reality. He could feel the warmth of her hands against his skin, hear the soft murmur of her prayers as they wrapped around him like a protective blanket.

At last, the tide of battle began to turn, and the sound of retreating enemies echoed through the dusty air.

With the fighting finally quelled, Darius was lifted and carried to a makeshift triage within the cavern.

Days passed in a blur of pain and healing, and during that time, Kyra stayed by his side. She refused to leave him, her heart entwined with his in a way that felt almost ethereal. Darius gradually regained consciousness, and with it, he felt the strength of her presence radiating warmth and light, dispelling the darkness that had threatened to engulf him.

When he finally opened his eyes, he found Kyra sitting beside him, her eyes red from worry but shining with relief. "Darius," she breathed, her voice trembling. "You're awake."

"Kyra..." he managed, his voice hoarse. "You're here."

"Always," she replied, tears of joy spilling down her cheeks as she leaned closer. "You scared me. I thought-"

"You thought what?" he interrupted, his voice stronger now as he reached out, brushing his fingers against her cheek. "You thought I wouldn't make it?"

Her gaze locked onto his, and in that moment, all the barriers they had built crumbled away. "I thought I'd lose you. I couldn't bear the thought of a world without you in it."

Darius's heart swelled at her words, and he pulled her closer, their foreheads resting against each other as the weight of their shared experience hung in the air. "You're my light, Kyra. I fought to come back to you."

Tears streamed down her face as she nodded. "And I prayed for you. I realized... I realized how deeply I care for you, how much you mean to me."

In that vulnerable moment, Darius leaned in, capturing her lips with his, a kiss that held all the unspoken love and longing they had kept hidden for too long. It was a tender exploration, a promise of what was to come, and they poured everything they felt into that kiss-fear, relief, hope, and love.

As the kiss deepened, the air around them crackled with an undeniable energy. Darius carefully pulled Kyra into his embrace, the world outside fading as they melted into one another. She tasted like warmth and safety, and for Darius, the battle, the pain, and the chaos melted away, leaving only the truth of their hearts.

Kyra's hands tangled in his hair as the kiss grew more passionate, igniting a fire within them both.

Darius's hands roamed her back, pulling her closer as they lost themselves in the moment. The lingering scent of incense from the cavern mixed with the warmth of their bodies, creating an atmosphere thick with desire and longing.

Time became irrelevant as they surrendered to each other completely. The love that had simmered beneath the surface erupted into a blaze, consuming them with its intensity. They found solace in each other's arms, a sanctuary amid the aftermath of war.

When they finally pulled away, breathless and wide-eyed, the reality of what had just transpired settled over them. The bond they had formed through shared experiences, trials, and tribulations had solidified into something unbreakable.

"Darius..." Kyra began, her cheeks flushed. "What does this mean for us?"

Darius brushed his thumb across her lips, a soft smile on his face. "It means we fight for each other now, Kyra. We fight for our love and for Kandahar.

Together."

With those words, they sealed their fate, not just as warriors of Kandahar but as partners intertwined in the dance of love and life. In a world fraught with uncertainty, they found strength in each other, ready to face whatever challenges lay ahead, united by a love that had risen from the ashes of battle.

Chapter 10 - Ties of Blood and Empire

The aftermath of the battle left Kandahar both scarred and resilient. Darius had regained his strength, and with Kyra at his side, they began to work towards rebuilding the city they loved. The air was heavy with the scent of fresh earth, a promise of renewal amidst the devastation. However, the unity forged in the flames of war was not without its complications.

While Darius and Kyra found solace in their burgeoning love, Aryanath grappled with the changes swirling around him. He had always viewed Kyra as more than just a friend; she had been his confidante, the one person who understood the weight of their shared past. As a child, he had often been lost in the labyrinth of his family's expectations, but Kyra had been a beacon of light, a spirit partner who had always been there to support him.

Now, as he observed the connection between Kyra and Darius-an unbreakable bond that seemed to deepen with every glance and touch—he felt an ache in his chest. The knowledge that she had chosen Darius, a man who had fought valiantly yet was still an outsider to their bloodline, was like a bitter pill to swallow.

One evening, Aryanath found himself wandering through the remnants of the city. The sounds of laughter and rebuilding echoed in the distance, but he felt an unsettling solitude wrap around him.

Memories of his childhood with Kyra flooded his mind—her laughter as they raced through the fields, her unwavering determination in the face of adversity, and the warmth of her hand in his as they shared their dreams.

He could almost hear her voice in the wind, calling out to him with that familiar lilt that had always brought him comfort. But now, he felt an

insurmountable distance between them, a divide that was rooted not only in love but in their respective destinies.

Lost in thought, Aryanath made his way to the temple, where he found Kyra and Darius deep in conversation. They were seated together, their faces illuminated by the soft glow of the candles flickering around them. Darius's hand rested gently on Kyra's, a simple yet intimate gesture that struck Aryanath like a blow.

He hesitated in the doorway, a mix of emotions churning within him. He had always known this day might come, but witnessing it unfold before his eyes felt like a cruel twist of fate. Steeling himself, he stepped into the room, forcing a smile that didn't quite reach his eyes.

"Kyra, Darius," he greeted, his voice steadier than he felt. "I hope I'm not interrupting."

Kyra looked up, her expression brightening as she saw him. "Aryanath! Not at all. We were just discussing the plans for the next phase of rebuilding."

Darius nodded, his demeanor open and friendly. "We could use your insights. This city has always thrived because of its leadership, and your perspective is invaluable."

But Aryanath felt his heart sink. He appreciated Darius's words, but the knowledge of his feelings for Kyra lingered heavily in the air. "Of course," he replied, forcing himself to focus on the task at hand.

"Let's not waste time, then."

As they discussed strategies and priorities, Aryanath couldn't shake the feeling that he was an intruder in a space that had once felt like home. He watched as Kyra leaned into Darius, their laughter punctuating the air like a sweet melody, while he fought to maintain his composure. Every smile they exchanged cut deeper, igniting an old jealousy he had thought he had outgrown.

Later that evening, Aryanath found himself outside the temple, the cool night air a stark contrast to the warmth inside. The stars twinkled overhead, a reminder of the endless possibilities life held, yet he felt trapped in a moment he couldn't escape.

He closed his eyes, memories of Kyra flooding back— her childhood dreams of adventure, her fierce loyalty to their home, and the way they had shared everything. He could still remember the promise they had made as children, pledging to stand together against the world, never to let anything come between them. But now, it felt as if the tides had shifted, and he was left standing on the shore, watching as the waves carried her further away.

A few moments later, Kyra stepped outside, her face illuminated by the moonlight. "Aryanath?" she called softly, concern etched on her features. "Are you okay?"

He turned to face her, swallowing hard as he fought to maintain his composure. "I'm fine, just... lost in thought."

Kyra took a step closer, sensing the turmoil beneath his calm exterior. "You don't seem fine. Is it about the battle? About Kandahar?"

"It's about everything," he admitted, his voice low.

"About how things have changed between us."

"Things have changed, yes," she said gently, her eyes searching his. "But I thought we were still connected.

You are my friend in every way that matters."

"Are we, Kyra?" he asked, the question hanging heavily between them. "What about Darius? You've chosen him, and I can't help but feel... forgotten."

Her eyes widened, and she took a step closer, reaching for his hand. "You're not forgotten! You're so important to me. Darius... he's different. He fought for Kandahar, for our future, and I respect him deeply. But you-our bond, our history-it's irreplaceable."

Aryanath felt a flicker of hope, but it was quickly overshadowed by a pang of sadness. "I want you to be happy, Kyra. But I can't shake the feeling that I've lost you."

She shook her head, her voice firm. "You haven't lost me. I still need you, Aryanath. But this-what's between Darius and me—it's something I never expected. It's real, and it's growing."

"Do you love him?" Aryanath's voice cracked, vulnerability spilling into the night.

Kyra paused, the weight of her emotions clear in her eyes. "I do. But my love for you is different, Aryanath. You are my childhood, my home. This is new territory for me."

The two stood in silence, the air thick with unspoken words. Aryanath longed to pull her into his arms, to shield her from the complications of love and loyalty, but he knew he had to respect her feelings. "I just wish things could go back to how they were," he finally admitted, his voice barely above a whisper.

"I wish that too," she replied, tears glistening in her eyes. "But the world is changing. We must adapt."

In that moment, Aryanath felt a surge of protective instinct rise within him. "Then let me help you navigate this. We're stronger together, and I refuse to let our bond fade just because you've found love with Darius."

Kyra nodded, gratitude shining in her eyes. "Thank you, Aryanath. I promise, I will never abandon you."

As they stood there, a fragile understanding settled between them, one that acknowledged the complexities of love, friendship, and family.

Aryanath knew that the path ahead would be challenging, but he was determined to remain a part of Kyra's life, no matter how complicated their emotions became.

That night, as the stars twinkled overhead, Aryanath resolved to be a steadfast ally for both Kyra and Darius, even as his heart ached with unrequited feelings. The ties of blood and empire were intricate, but his loyalty to Kyra would remain unshakable, as he navigated the uncharted waters of love, friendship, and destiny in a world that had forever changed.

Chapter 11 - The Price of Loyalty

The aftermath of the Battle of Arachosia left a deep mark on the hearts of those who remained in Kandahar. As rebuilding efforts progressed, the tension between loyalty, love, and ambition became increasingly palpable. Darius and Kyra stood at the center of this emotional storm, their bond growing stronger yet more complicated with every passing day.

Darius had taken on the mantle of a leader, working tirelessly to ensure the safety and prosperity of Kandahar. His admiration for Kyra fueled his dedication, as her unwavering spirit inspired him to fight for a brighter future. They spent long hours strategizing together, sharing both laughter and moments of vulnerability. With each plan discussed, their connection deepened, leading to intimate moments where their hands would linger together, and stolen kisses became a precious part of their routine.

One evening, as the sun dipped below the horizon, casting a warm golden hue over the city, Darius and Kyra found themselves alone in the cavern. The soft glow of the candles created an intimate ambiance, enhancing the feelings that simmered between them.

Darius stepped closer, his eyes locked onto Kyra's, his heart racing as he brushed a strand of hair behind her ear.

"Kyra," he murmured, his voice low and filled with longing. "Every moment with you feels like a dream.

I never want to wake up."

Kyra's breath caught in her throat as Darius's fingers grazed her cheek. The warmth of his touch ignited a fire within her, drawing her closer to him. "Darius, we can't let the world outside dictate how we feel," she whispered, her gaze flickering to the door as if fearing they might be interrupted.

His hand cupped her face as he leaned in, their lips almost touching. "Let them try. I will protect you, no matter the cost."

In that moment, the air crackled with electricity.

Their lips finally met in a passionate kiss, igniting a wave of desire that swept through both of them. It was a kiss that spoke of unspoken promises, a shared dream of a life beyond the battles and betrayals that surrounded them. As they embraced, the world outside faded into nothingness.

But just as the moment deepened, a loud crash echoed through the temple, breaking the spell. Both Darius and Kyra pulled apart, breathless, their hearts racing. They turned to see Aryanath standing in the doorway, his expression a mixture of shock and something else-hurt?

"Aryanath!" Kyra exclaimed, stepping away from Darius, her cheeks flushed. "I didn't expect to see you here."

"I can see that," he replied, his tone cold but the hurt in his eyes unmistakable. "I came to discuss the plans for the next phase of the reconstruction."

Darius crossed his arms, trying to mask the tension that crackled in the air. "We were just discussing strategies, Aryanath. There's no need to be confrontational."

But Aryanath's gaze was fixed on Kyra, his expression softening slightly as he stepped closer.

"Kyra, I need you to understand that your safety is paramount. Darius is an outsider, no matter how brave he is."

Kyra felt a pang of guilt at his words, yet her heart raced for Darius. "But Darius has proven himself time and again. He fought for Kandahar, for us!"

"That doesn't change the fact that he's not one of us," Aryanath insisted, his voice rising. "And while you may feel safe with him, the ties of blood and loyalty run deeper than you realize."

Kyra's eyes narrowed. "Are you suggesting that I shouldn't trust him? That I shouldn't follow my heart?"

Darius stepped forward, his tone firm. "I would never betray you, Kyra. You know that."

Before the argument could escalate further, a figure appeared in the doorway-Zarif, a merchant known for his dubious dealings. "Apologies for interrupting, but it seems there's a matter of great importance at hand," he announced, a sly smile creeping across his lips.

"What do you want, Zarif?" Aryanath asked, his irritation palpable.

Zarif's gaze shifted between them, sensing the tension. "I come bearing news that might change the course of this city. There are whispers of a conspiracy brewing among the remnants of the empire. Those who wish to see Kandahar fall are gathering strength."

Darius exchanged a worried glance with Kyra and Aryanath. "What do you mean? Who are they?"

"Old allies, enemies of the empire that once ruled this land. They seek to reclaim their territory and have plans to invade. They know of your vulnerabilities—your love, your alliances," Zarif replied, his voice lowering as if sharing a dangerous secret.

Kyra felt a chill run down her spine, her thoughts racing. "But we can't let them succeed. We must unite the people of Kandahar against this threat."

"Precisely," Darius agreed, his hand tightening around Kyra's. "We need to take action now."

But as they strategized, Aryanath remained silent, his mind a whirlpool of emotions. He watched the dynamic between Darius and Kyra, the bond they shared becoming more evident by the second. A rush of jealousy and protective instincts surged through him, battling against his desire to support his childhood friend.

Later that night, Aryanath found himself outside under the stars, his heart heavy with the weight of unspoken words. He remembered his childhood with Kyra, how they had shared everything-dreams, fears, and even secrets. But now, he felt a divide growing between them, one that he couldn't bridge.

As he stood lost in thought, Kyra emerged, her expression softening when she spotted him. "Aryanath, can we talk?"

"Talk?" he echoed, trying to mask the hurt in his voice. "About what? Your love for Darius?"

"About us," she replied, stepping closer. "About our friendship. I don't want to lose that."

"But you're choosing him," he said, the pain evident.

"What does that mean for us?"

Kyra hesitated, her heart aching at the thought of hurting him. "It means that I care for both of you in different ways. Darius is... something new for me.

But you've always been my rock, my anchor. I can't lose that."

Aryanath clenched his jaw, his emotions threatening to spill over. "And what if Darius isn't who he seems?

What if he turns against us?"

"Don't say that!" she urged, her eyes shining with unshed tears. "Darius would never betray us."

But in that moment, a slight flicker of doubt crept into her heart. The words of Zarif echoed in her mind, and she couldn't shake the feeling that danger was closing in. She reached out to Aryanath, desperate for reassurance. "I need you to trust me, Aryanath. Trust that I know what I'm doing."

His gaze softened, but the hurt remained. "I'll always trust you, Kyra. But I fear for what lies ahead."

As they stood together, an unexpected moment of intimacy ignited between them. Aryanath leaned closer, wrapping his arms around Kyra in a protective embrace. She melted against him, warmth spreading through her, and for a fleeting moment, it felt as though they were children again, sharing secrets under the starlit sky.

Yet, in the back of her mind, her thoughts wandered to Darius, and the connection they had forged. The heat of Aryanath's embrace ignited conflicting emotions within her—an intense pull toward both men who held pieces of her heart.

Meanwhile, inside the temple, Darius sensed the tension between Aryanath and Kyra, and a flicker of concern gripped him. He stepped outside, determined to confront whatever was brewing in the air. As he approached, he caught sight of Kyra in Aryanath's arms, their faces inches apart. Jealousy flared within him, but he pushed it aside, reminding himself of the stakes.

"Kyra," Darius called, his voice firm yet tender. "We need to focus on the threat facing Kandahar."

She pulled away from Aryanath, a mix of emotions washing over her. "I know, Darius. We're trying to figure things out."

Darius stepped closer, his gaze intense as he took her hands in his. "I won't let anything come between us.

We're stronger together, and I'll do whatever it takes to protect you."

Kyra felt the heat radiating from his touch, and despite the turmoil in her heart, she leaned in closer to Darius, drawn to him like a moth to a flame. "I trust you, Darius. Together, we'll face whatever comes our way."

The atmosphere crackled with unspoken tension as Darius leaned in to capture her lips once more and placing a peck on her lips, the kiss igniting the passion they shared. Aryanath watched, a mix of longing and hurt swirling within him. He had lost her to a love that felt destined, while he remained tethered to the past they once shared.

As Darius and Kyra embraced, Aryanath turned away, his heart heavy with the price of loyalty. He knew he had to protect them, even if it meant sacrificing his own happiness. The battle lines were drawn—not just against the impending threat of invaders but also within the tangled web of love, friendship, and loyalty that would ultimately shape their fates in the days to come.

But as shadows danced around them, the ties of blood and empire tightened, and the price of loyalty threatened to tear them apart, even as they fought to keep their love alive in a world filled with uncertainty.

Chapter 12 - Fate of the Prophecy

The sun dipped low on the horizon, casting an orange glow over the bustling streets of Kandahar.

The city, once a beacon of culture and unity, was now enveloped in an atmosphere of uncertainty. With the whispers of an impending invasion still echoing in the air, Darius had slipped away under the cover of night, determined to uncover the identity of the spy behind the conspiracy that threatened their lives and the safety of the city he had come to love.

Kyra felt a hollow ache in her heart as she watched him leave, a feeling compounded by the mounting tension with Aryanath. Darius had assured her that he would return, but as the days dragged on into weeks, the uncertainty gnawed at her. Each sunset that painted the skies red reminded her of the fire in Darius's eyes when he spoke of their dreams together. But now, those dreams felt like fragile wisps of smoke.

In the absence of Darius, Aryanath stepped up, his presence a comforting, albeit complicated, solace for Kyra. He was there every day, helping her navigate the chaos of rebuilding their community while assuaging her fears about Darius. "I promise you, Kyra, I will protect you. You are safe with me," he assured her one evening as they sat on the steps of the temple, the flickering lanterns casting gentle shadows around them.

"Thank you, Aryanath. It means so much to have you here," Kyra replied, her voice soft, but her heart was heavy with doubt. She had always cherished Aryanath, their bond stretching back to childhood, but the feelings had shifted. Each moment they spent together reminded her of the love she felt for Darius, which only complicated her feelings for Aryanath.

But as Aryanath's assurances grew more fervent, a dark seed of doubt began to take root in Kyra's mind.

"What if Darius is the threat?" he had suggested one night, his voice low, as though he feared the shadows would carry his words away. "He knows our plans."

The thought shook Kyra to her core. The very idea that Darius, the man she had entrusted with her heart, could be connected to the betrayal made her stomach churn. "No! Darius would never do that," she protested, desperation creeping into her voice.

But as the days passed, the whispers of Aryanath's doubts began to echo in her mind.

The weeks stretched on with every sunrise seeming to dim the light in her heart. She spent countless nights tossing and turning, replaying memories of Darius's warm laughter and unwavering resolve. She had faith in him, yet with each passing day, the uncertainty became more unbearable.

Finally, on the fourteenth day, a commotion outside the temple stirred her from a restless slumber. Heart racing, she dashed to the entrance, her breath hitching as she spotted a familiar silhouette approaching through the dusty haze of the evening light. Darius!

A wave of relief washed over her, banishing the doubts that had plagued her for so long. She rushed to him, throwing her arms around his neck as he lifted her off the ground, spinning her in a joyful embrace. "You're back!" she exclaimed, her voice muffled against his shoulder.

Darius set her down gently, his eyes gleaming with the intensity of their shared longing. "I'm sorry it took so long, Kyra. There was so much to uncover, and I couldn't return until I had answers."

"Tell me everything," she urged, stepping back to look into his eyes, searching for any hint of deceit.

But all she found was sincerity.

"I'll explain later, but for now, we need to be cautious. The spy is closer than we think, and there are those who wish to see us fail," he replied, urgency lacing his tone.

"Are you okay?" Kyra asked, brushing her fingers over the dark stubble on his jaw, noting the weariness in his eyes. "You look exhausted."

"I'm fine, just... weary from the journey," he said, and she could sense the weight of what he carried. "I missed you more than I can say."

Her heart fluttered at his words. In that moment, the chaos of their surroundings faded, and all that mattered was the two of them. "I'm so glad you're back, Darius. I.." she hesitated, the words caught in her throat. "I was so worried."

"Worried about me, or about what I might find?" he asked gently, his gaze probing yet tender.

"About both," she admitted, biting her lip as she stepped closer, the space between them crackling with tension. "And about what Aryanath said..."

Darius's expression darkened, a flicker of anger flashing in his eyes. "Aryanath is protective, but he doesn't understand. I would never betray you or this city."

"I know that," she said, reaching out to touch his cheek. "But the days without you were so difficult. I kept wondering if I could trust that you would come back to me."

In that moment, the tension that had built up between them broke, replaced by the raw need they had both been holding at bay. Darius cupped her face in his hands, his thumb brushing her cheek softly as he leaned in, capturing her lips in a fervent kiss. It was a kiss filled with longing, desperation, and love that poured out like a flood, washing away the doubts and fears.

As their lips moved together, Kyra felt the world around them vanish. Darius pulled her closer, deepening the kiss, igniting a fire within her that she thought had been smothered during his absence. She melted against him, surrendering to the sensations that swept over her as he kissed her with a hunger that left her breathless.

Breaking apart, they leaned their foreheads together, gasping for breath, their hearts racing in unison.

"I've missed you," Kyra whispered, her voice barely audible, filled with emotion.

"Every moment away from you felt like an eternity," Darius replied, his voice thick with longing. "But I need you to understand, Kyra: I returned not just for our love, but to protect everything we hold dear."

Her heart swelled at his words, but the reality of their situation crashed back over her like a wave.

"What about Aryanath? He... he's worried about you, about us."

Darius's expression hardened slightly. "Aryanath means well, but his jealousy could be a danger. We can't let him distract us from the real threat."

The tension of the past weeks hung between them, but the warmth of their connection provided a sanctuary amid the storm. They shared another kiss, more tender now, exploring the depths of their feelings, seeking solace in each other.

After a few moments, Kyra stepped back, her breath hitching as she looked up at Darius. "So what did you find out? Who is behind the spy?"

Darius's expression turned serious as he stepped back, pulling away from their embrace. "It's more complicated than we thought. The spy is someone within our own ranks, feeding information to the would-be invaders. I need to gather the council and strategize, but I wanted to see you first."

Kyra nodded, the gravity of his words settling in. "I'll help you in any way I can."

"Your safety is my priority," Darius replied, his voice firm yet gentle. "But right now, we need to prepare for what's to come. The prophecy that binds our fates has not yet revealed its full power."

As they stood together, the weight of their shared burden hung over them, yet the warmth of their love ignited a flame of hope. They would face the shadows lurking on the horizon, but together, they would find the strength to combat whatever fate had in store for them.

With their hearts entwined and their spirits ready to fight, Kyra and Darius stepped into the unknown, prepared to confront not only the threat to Kandahar but also the deeper connection that tied them together, revealing that sometimes, love could rise from the ashes of uncertainty, igniting a new destiny in its wake.

Chapter 13 - Legacy of the Mortals

The sun rose over Kandahar, casting a golden hue across the ancient city, its rays illuminating the rich tapestry of history that surrounded them. Darius stood atop the citadel, surveying the landscape, the air thick with anticipation. The past weeks had been tumultuous, yet they had brought him to this moment—a turning point that could either save their legacy or shatter it.

As the council gathered below, the tension in the air was palpable. Darius had spent countless hours piecing together the threads of betrayal that had woven through their ranks. After an exhaustive investigation, he had finally uncovered the identity of the spy—an ally turned adversary, someone he had once trusted completely. His heart raced as he remembered the conversations, the shared laughter, and the promises made. Now, it was time to reveal the truth.

"Ladies and gentlemen," he began, his voice strong and steady, "we stand at a crossroads, where the shadows of betrayal threaten our beloved Kandahar.

The spy among us is none other than Zarif. He has been leaking our plans to the enemy, using his position to sow discord and strife."

A collective gasp rippled through the crowd as Darius continued, "Zarif sought to destroy our unity for his gain, but together, we will not let his treachery define us." The murmurs of disbelief began to dissipate, replaced by a growing sense of resolve.

With a swift motion, Darius gestured for Zarif to step forward. The once-respected merchant now appeared small and frightened, the weight of his actions pressing down on him. "You have betrayed your people, Zarif. For that, you will answer to the council. We must cleanse our ranks of this treachery if we are to save our legacy."

As the guards approached to escort Zarif away, the atmosphere shifted, replaced with a renewed sense of determination among the people. Darius felt a surge of pride for his home, the resilience of its people igniting a flame of hope in his heart. They were bound together, ready to fight for their future and the legacy of Kandahar.

Later that evening, as the sun dipped below the horizon, painting the sky in hues of pink and orange, Darius returned to Kyra. She was in their shared sanctuary, a space filled with fragrant blossoms and soft fabrics, the remnants of their love mingling with the anticipation of what was to come.

"Kyra," he said softly, stepping toward her, feeling the weight of the day lift as he gazed into her eyes.

"We did it. We've uncovered the spy, and Kandahar is safe once more."

A smile broke across her face, illuminating her features, and Darius felt his heart swell with love.

But it wasn't just the triumph that stirred his emotions; it was the undeniable connection they shared. As he moved closer, he noticed something in her eyes, a glimmer of joy mixed with something deeper.

"Darius," she began, her voice trembling slightly.

"There's something I need to tell you."

His heart raced as he stepped even closer. "What is it, Kyra?"

"I'm... I'm pregnant," she whispered, the words hanging in the air like a beautiful promise. The world around them faded as the realization washed over him, filling him with an overwhelming sense of joy.

"Pregnant?" he echoed, a smile breaking across his face, disbelief and elation intertwining. "We're going to be parents?"

Kyra nodded, her eyes shimmering with unshed tears of happiness. Darius stepped forward, pulling her into an embrace that felt like home. "This is the happiest moment of my life," he said, his voice thick with emotion as he kissed her tenderly.

He gently placed his hands on her belly, feeling the warmth radiating from within her. "I promise to protect you both," he vowed, his heart overflowing with love and commitment. "We will build a life together, a legacy that carries our names through the ages."

As they stood entwined in each other's arms, the weight of their responsibilities faded, leaving only the pure joy of the life they were about to create.

In the days that followed, the atmosphere in Kandahar shifted. With the threat of invasion quelled and the bond between Darius and Kyra strengthened, preparations for their wedding ceremony began in earnest. The entire city buzzed with excitement as artisans crafted intricate decorations and local chefs prepared sumptuous feasts, eager to celebrate the love that had blossomed amid the chaos.

Kyra worked tirelessly alongside the women of the community, weaving delicate garlands of flowers that would adorn the temple where they would exchange their vows. Laughter filled the air as they shared stories and dreams of the future, the bond of sisterhood weaving them together like the colorful threads in the garlands they crafted.

Darius was no less dedicated, rallying the men of Kandahar to prepare for the celebration. They erected a grand canopy beneath which he and Kyra would unite, their love a beacon of hope for all who had witnessed the trials they had overcome.

On the day of the ceremony, the sun shone brightly, illuminating the temple with a warm glow. Darius stood before the gathered crowd, his heart pounding in his chest as he awaited Kyra's arrival. There was a soft breeze, each moment stretching into eternity as he envisioned the life they would share.

When Kyra finally appeared, dressed in a flowing floral gown adorned with intricate embroidery that caught the light, Darius's breath caught in his throat.

She was stunning, radiating a beauty that transcended time. The gentle sway of her movements captivated him, and for a moment, he felt as though the world had faded away, leaving only the two of them.

As she reached him, their eyes locked, and the world around them vanished. With the blessings of their community surrounding them, they exchanged vows, promising to stand by each other through every challenge life would throw their way.

When Darius took her hands in his, he felt the warmth of her love and the new life growing within her. "I will always protect you, Kyra. You are my heart, my soul, and the mother of our child," he declared, his voice strong and unwavering.

Tears glistened in Kyra's eyes as she smiled, her heart overflowing with love. "And I will cherish you, Darius, for all that you are and all that we will build together."

As they sealed their promises with a kiss, the crowd erupted into cheers, the sound echoing through the streets of Kandahar, a celebration of love, unity, and the legacy they would create together.

In that moment, Darius understood the true meaning of legacy-not just the name they would pass down through generations, but the love and strength that would sustain them through every challenge.

Together, they would forge a future filled with hope, courage, and an unbreakable bond, destined to endure the test of time.

As the days turned into weeks following the joyous union of Kyra and Darius, Aryanath found himself observing the couple from a distance, a mix of emotions swirling within him. He had always held a deep affection for Kyra, their shared childhood memories a treasure trove of laughter and dreams.

Yet, as he watched her with Darius, he began to understand the profound bond that had blossomed between them—a connection that transcended mere friendship.

Every glance, every touch between Kyra and Darius resonated with an intensity that was impossible to ignore. The way they moved together, their laughter echoing in the air, spoke of a love that was genuine and unyielding. Aryanath felt a pang in his heart, but it was quickly replaced by a sense of acceptance. He realized that true love was not about possession but about witnessing the happiness of those we care for.

One afternoon, Aryanath visited Kyra and Darius's home, where the atmosphere was filled with warmth and laughter. The couple was preparing for the arrival of their child, and they were filled with excitement. As he stepped inside, he was greeted by the sight of Kyra arranging tiny garments made of soft fabric, her face aglow with happiness. Darius was nearby, engaged in a playful conversation with her, his eyes sparkling with affection.

"Look at this one, Aryanath!" Kyra exclaimed, holding up a small garment embroidered with intricate designs. "I can't wait to see our little one in this!"

Aryanath felt a swell of emotion as he watched her.

She was radiant, and in that moment, he understood that her happiness was intertwined with Darius's presence. "It suits you both," he replied, forcing a smile that masked the bittersweet feelings within.

As the afternoon unfolded, Aryanath listened to the couple share their hopes and dreams for their family.

They spoke of their plans for the future, envisioning a home filled with love, laughter, and adventure.

Darius often turned to Kyra with an adoration that made Aryanath's heart ache, yet he couldn't help but feel a sense of joy for her. This was what she had always wanted—a family, a partner who cherished her, and a life filled with love.

Later, as the sun began to set, casting a saffron glow through the windows, Aryanath found a moment alone with Kyra. He approached her, his expression earnest. "You know, I've always admired you, Kyra," he began, searching for the right words. "But seeing you with Darius... it makes me realize just how deeply you're loved. And if anyone deserves that, it's you."

Kyra's smile widened, and her eyes glistened with gratitude. "Thank you, Aryanath. Your support means the world to me. Darius makes me happier than I ever thought possible. I can feel it in every moment we share."

In that instant, Aryanath felt a profound sense of clarity wash over him. The bond Kyra shared with Darius was something he had longed for her to find.

He wanted her happiness, even if it meant stepping back from his own desires. "I'm genuinely happy for you both. You're starting a new family, and I can see the joy it brings you."

Their conversation deepened as they reminisced about their childhood, the dreams they had once shared. Aryanath realized that while his feelings for Kyra were steeped in the past, her future was unfolding beautifully before him. She was embarking on a journey filled with love and promise, and that was enough for him.

As he left their home that evening, Aryanath felt a sense of peace settle in his heart. He had come to terms with the reality of their relationship, knowing that sometimes, true love meant letting go. Kyra's happiness was paramount, and witnessing her embrace her new life with Darius filled him with a bittersweet joy. He would always cherish the memories they had created together, but now, he looked forward to seeing her thrive in this new chapter of her life, proud to be a part of her journey as a friend and ally.

Chapter 14 - The Arrival of Vajra

After thirty-eight weeks filled with anticipation, hope, and dreams of a future together, the moment finally arrived. Kyra's labor began with the first rays of dawn breaking over Kandahar, painting the sky in hues of pink and gold. The air was charged with a mixture of excitement and nervous energy as Darius held her hand, whispering words of encouragement and love.

The hours passed slowly, each contraction a testament to Kyra's strength and resilience. Darius remained by her side, unwavering in his support, his heart racing with every heartbeat they shared. The pain was immense, but so was the promise of new life. As the sun climbed higher, filling their sanctuary with warmth, Kyra summoned the last reserves of her strength.

With a final push and a cry that echoed through the room, their daughter was born. Darius's breath caught in his throat as the midwife placed the tiny bundle in Kyra's arms. Tears of joy streamed down her face, mingling with the sweat and exhaustion of the long hours. Darius gently leaned forward, planting a soft kiss on Kyra's forehead, filled with love and gratitude. "You've completed me in every way," he murmured, his voice thick with emotion.

He carefully took their daughter from Kyra's arms, cradling her against his chest. "The torchbearer of Kandahar is here," he declared, a smile breaking across his face as he gazed into the tiny face of their newborn. Her eyes, bright and curious, seemed to hold the promise of greatness.

Kyra watched with a mixture of pride and love, her heart swelling at the sight of Darius embracing their daughter. "We name her Vajra," she said softly, the name carrying weight and significance. "May she embody strength and resilience, a true daughter of Kandahar."

Darius nodded, feeling the gravity of the moment.

"Our descendants will follow her preaching and command," he vowed, the conviction in his voice unwavering. He felt a surge of hope for the future, knowing that Vajra would carry the legacy of their love and the spirit of their people.

As they held their daughter together, a sense of peace enveloped them. They were no longer just Kyra and Darius; they were a family, bound together by love and shared dreams. In that moment, surrounded by the whispers of their ancestors and the promise of the future, they understood the true meaning of legacy-one that would live on through Vajra, the embodiment of their hopes and aspirations for Kandahar.

With each passing moment, they felt the weight of their responsibilities as parents, but they also felt the joy of new beginnings. They were ready to guide Vajra, to teach her the ways of their ancestors, and to instill in her the values that had been the foundation of their love and their land.

As the day turned to evening, Darius and Kyra sat together, their daughter nestled safely between them.

The sun dipped below the horizon, casting a warm glow over the city they loved. In that tranquil moment, they knew that they had begun a new chapter, one filled with love, hope, and the **Legacy of Vajra**-*Kandahar's torchbearer, destined to illuminate the path for generations to come.*

Chapter 15 - The Princess of Kandahar

Nineteen years had passed since the birth of Vajra, and in that time, she had blossomed into a remarkable young woman. The streets of Kandahar echoed with her laughter, a sound that carried the warmth of the sun and the promise of a bright future. As the daughter of Kyra and Darius, Vajra bore the best qualities of her parents—a fierce spirit tempered with compassion, and a sharp intellect balanced by a deep love for her people.

Kyra and Darius watched with pride as their daughter took on the mantle of leadership. Vajra had grown up amidst the teachings of the great warriors and scholars of Kandahar. Her days were filled with lessons from wise elders, combat training from seasoned fighters, and discussions on governance from her father, Darius. And she learned about her people and their history from her mother. She absorbed knowledge like a sponge, and each lesson only sharpened her natural talents.

The temple that once stood as a testament to Alexander the Great's legacy was now a sanctuary for the ideals of peace and unity that Darius and Kyra had instilled in their family. It was a place where Vajra often sought solace, reflecting on her duties and the future of her beloved Kandahar. The temple had been preserved with care, its stones bearing witness to the strength and resilience of those who came before her.

Now, as she prepared to join the council, Vajra felt the weight of expectation resting on her shoulders.

She stood before the mirror, taking in the image of the young woman she had become. Her hair cascaded like a dark river down her back, and her striking eyes-so reminiscent of Darius—held a determination that spoke of her unwavering resolve.

Today was not just another day; it was the day she would step into the world of leadership.

With a deep breath, Vajra made her way to the council chamber, where the elders awaited her. As she entered, the room fell silent, the atmosphere charged with anticipation. Aryanath, their steadfast advisor and a loyal warrior, stood at the forefront, his presence a reassuring anchor for both Vajra and the council. He had become a mentor to her, sharing stories of valor and honor that inspired her to stand tall in her convictions.

"Princess Vajra," Aryanath greeted her with a respectful nod, his expression a blend of pride and affection. "Today marks a significant moment for Kandahar. We are honored to welcome you into the council."

The elders acknowledged her with nods of approval, their eyes twinkling with the memories of her childhood.

Vajra felt a swell of emotion; she had always admired these individuals, learning from their wisdom and experience. Now, she was ready to contribute her voice to the discussions that would shape the future of their land.

"Thank you," she said, her voice steady and clear. "It is an honor to stand before you today, ready to serve my people and uphold the legacy of Kandahar."

As she took her seat among the council members, Vajra felt a sense of belonging. The council room was adorned with tapestries depicting the rich history of Kandahar-the great battles fought, the alliances forged, and the moments of peace celebrated. Each image reminded her of the responsibilities she now bore.

In the days that followed, Vajra immersed herself in the affairs of the kingdom. She actively participated in discussions on trade agreements, defense strategies, and community welfare. Her voice, once soft and hesitant, grew stronger as she expressed her thoughts and ideas. The council members quickly recognized her intelligence and passion, often seeking her opinion on matters that affected their people.

Kyra and Darius watched with pride as their daughter flourished in her role. They had worked tirelessly to ensure that Kandahar remained a safe haven, a place where dreams could thrive and hopes could flourish. Their love for each other had woven a tapestry of strength, and they saw that same fabric reflected in Vajra.

One evening, after a long day of council meetings, the family gathered in their home. Kyra shared tales of their ancestors, emphasizing the importance of unity and resilience. Darius added his own stories of the challenges they had faced and overcome together.

Their words inspired Vajra, fueling her determination to honor their legacy.

"I feel so proud to be a part of this lineage," Vajra said, her voice filled with emotion. "You both have shown me what it means to lead with love and integrity. I will do my best to make you proud."

"You already do," Darius replied, placing a reassuring hand on her shoulder. "You are the embodiment of our hopes for Kandahar. Your heart, your wisdom— these will guide you in your journey ahead."

As the sun set beyond the horizon, casting a warm glow over Kandahar, the family shared a moment of quiet reflection. They understood that the legacy they had built together would continue through Vajra, the Princess of Kandahar, destined to lead her people with the same love and dedication that had defined their lives.

With her parents by her side and the unwavering support of Aryanath, Vajra felt ready to embrace the challenges ahead. She knew that she would not only protect her home but also cultivate the spirit of unity and strength that had been the cornerstone of Kandahar's history. The future was bright, and the legacy of love and leadership would endure for generations to come.